SCOOBY-DOO!™

FIVE FAVOURITE SPOOKY STORIES

PEUK 5849

Published by Ladybird Books Ltd
A Penguin Company
Penguin Books Ltd, 80 Strand, London, WC2R ORL, England
Penguin Books Australia Ltd, Camberwell, Victoria, Australia
Penguin Group (NZ), 67 Apollo Drive, Mairangi Bay, Auckland, New Zealand

ISBN-13: 978-1-84646-612-0

2 4 6 8 10 9 7 5 3 1

Ladybird and the device of a ladybird are trademarks
of Ladybird Books Ltd

Printed in China

SCOOBY-DOO!™

FIVE FAVOURITE SPOOKY STORIES

CONTENTS

"Rrrrr! Brrrr!" Scooby-Doo and Shaggy hugged each other to keep warm.

"Like, it's freezing out here," said Shaggy.

"Well, it is winter," said Velma.

"And we are outside, waiting to ski," Daphne added.

"And you are eating ice cream," said Fred.

"Well, Scoob, old buddy. Let's get some hot dogs then!" Shaggy grinned.

"Rummy!" replied Scooby.

"Ski lodge, here we come!" said Shaggy.

"Not so fast!" said Fred. "We came to this mountain to ski. And that is what we are going to do."

"But we better do it fast," Velma said. "I heard there is a storm watch. If the snow gets bad, the mountain may close."

Velma, Fred and Daphne hopped onto the ski lift. "See you at the top!" said Daphne.

Then it was Shaggy and Scooby's turn.
"Oomph!" The bench crashed into them, and
they tumbled onto the seat.
"Going up!" said Shaggy.
The buddies glided over the trees to the top of
the mountain.

"Time to get off, good buddy," Shaggy said.
"Rokay," said Scooby.
"Ron, roo…ree!"
Scooby and Shaggy jumped off the ski lift.
"Wooooaaaaah!"
They slipped and slid and teetered and tottered off the path, and away from their friends. They couldn't stop.

Finally, they stumbled to a stop
– in front of another ski lodge.
"How about a rest?" said Shaggy.
"Reah!" said Scooby.
Shaggy grinned. "Groovy. We can
get those hot dogs now!"

Inside, the lodge was dark. Cobwebs hung
from the ceiling. Sheets covered tables.
And dust covered everything.

"There's no one here," said Shaggy,
disappointed. "No cooks or waiters."
He picked up a phone. "And no dial tone.
We can't even call for pizza."

Scooby padded into the kitchen.
"Yummy!" said Shaggy.
He opened a door. Out tumbled
popcorn and potato crisps.
"Eat first!" Shaggy shouted. "Ski later!"
Scooby ripped open one bag.
Shaggy ripped open another.

"C-r-e-a-k!" Shaggy stopped eating.
"What was that?"
"C-R-E-A-K!"
Slowly, slowly, the kitchen door swung open.
Slowly, slowly, the kitchen door swung closed.
"Whoooo!" A ghostly cry filled the air.

"Boom!" Something crashed upstairs. Shaggy dropped his popcorn. "Boom!" Scooby dropped his crisps. "Rhost!" shouted Scooby.

Shapes swirled outside the windows.
Bangs echoed through the lodge.
"Whoooo! Whoooo!"
"Like, it's not just one ghost!" Shaggy moaned.
"This place is crawling with ghosts!"

They ran for the door.

"Push!" said Shaggy. Scooby pushed. But the door wouldn't open.

"Rull!" Scooby said. Shaggy pulled. But the door still wouldn't open.

"We're trapped!" Shaggy cried.

They crawled under the table.
"Oh, why did we go off on
our own?" Shaggy sobbed.
"How are we going to get out?"

All at once, the door swung open. Great white
shapes floated inside.
"Zoinks! They're closing in!" said Shaggy.
One lifted an arm and pointed right at them.
"Raggy!" shouted Scooby. "Run!"

The buddies raced around the ghosts.

"Stop!" one commanded.

Shaggy skidded to a stop. The voice sounded
familiar.

"What are you guys doing?" asked another ghost.

"Are you okay?" asked the third.

"Velma?" said Shaggy. "Fred?"
"Raphne?" Scooby added.
Velma, Daphne and Fred shook off the snow
covering their heads, arms and legs.

"Of course it's us," said Fred. "We followed
your tracks to find you."
"We thought you were ghosts," Shaggy
explained, "and that this place was haunted."

"Whoooo! Whoooo! Boom! Crash!"
Shaggy jumped into Scooby's arms.
"See?" said Shaggy. "Listen to that!"
"The wind is making the 'whoooo' noise,"
Velma said.
"And the booms?" asked Shaggy.

"That's just tree branches hitting the roof," Daphne said.

Shaggy pointed to the white shapes outside the window. "Explain that!"

Fred laughed. "Easy. It's snow blowing around."

"But the door opened and closed by itself," said Shaggy. "Then it was stuck. This place really is haunted!"

Shaggy tried to run but slipped in a puddle of melted snow. "Don't be silly," said Velma. "The wind blew against the door so hard it wouldn't open."

Daphne patted Scooby. "The storm is really
bad. The mountain is closing."
Fred checked his watch. "We missed the last
ski lift run. What are we going to do now?"

Velma shrugged. "We can build a fire and wait right here."
Scooby gulped. "Rere?"
"This place gives me the creeps, but okay," Shaggy said, and he walked away.
"Raggy!" shouted Scooby.

"Like, cool it, good buddy," said Shaggy.
He pointed to the fire. "I'm just getting the
marshmallows!"

"See, guys, this ski lodge isn't so bad," said Velma.

"So long as we don't run out of marshmallows it's
cool. Right, Scooby?" Shaggy replied.

"Scooby-Dooby-Doo!"

The Mystery Machine squealed to a halt.
Velma jumped out. "We're late!" she cried.
"The Museum of Natural History will close
before we get to see the dinosaurs."
"Scoob and I are sorry, Velma,"
Shaggy said. "But like, we had
to stop for pizza."

MUSEUM
OF
NATURAL
HISTORY

"Don't worry, Velma," Daphne said.
"There is time to see the new show."
Fred looked at a map. "The Great Dinosaur
Hall is this way!"
"But the cafeteria is the other way!"
said Shaggy.

Velma led the gang through the jungle room.
Shaggy read a sign. "Gorillas in the wild."
"Ratch out!" Scooby shouted. A gorilla was
swinging right at them!

"Don't worry," said Velma. "These gorillas are
puppets. They are wired to move and make noises
so we can see how they live in a real jungle."
Shaggy sighed. "Like, I wish those bananas
were real."

Next the gang came to the elephants.
The animals raised their trunks.
"Rakes?" asked Scooby.
"Fakes!" said Velma.
"Even those peanuts!" said Shaggy.

Finally, they reached the Dinosaur Hall.
Large dinosaur skeletons peered down at them.
A crowd of people oohed and ahhed.

GREAT DINOSAUR HALL

"Look at that!" Velma said. "A brachiosaur – it looks so real!"

"Amazing!" said Fred. "Jeepers!" said Daphne.

"Rikes!" said Scooby. The brachiosaur looked too real. Its great jaws opened and closed. "I am starving," Shaggy said.

"Re too," said Scooby, licking his lips.

Shaggy turned to a security guard. "Like, where's the best place to chow down?" he asked.

"The cafeteria is this way," the guard said. He waved his arm, and hit a sign.

"Oops!" said the guard. "I have new glasses. And I still can't see very well. But I can take you to the cafeteria. I have to go that way to start closing the museum."

A few minutes later, Shaggy and Scooby had emptied the salad bar, the cold drink machines and everything in between.

All at once, the cafeteria lights flicked.
On, off. On, off.
Shouts echoed all around. Something was
happening!

"Come on, Scoob!" shouted
Shaggy. "We have to find
the others!"

They raced back to the Dinosaur Hall. One of the brachiosaur skeletons swung its mighty head. It snapped its jaws. One leg moved, then another.

"It's alive!" a boy shouted.

Everyone ran in fright.
"Don't panic!" Velma called. A shadow fell
over the gang. The dinosaur roared, right over
their heads.
"Run!" cried Fred.

They raced past the elephants.
The elephants raised their trunks
and stomped their feet.
They sounded angry.

Scooby and the gang sped past the gorillas.
The gorillas were swinging from vine to vine.
"Jinkies!" cried Velma. "What is going
on here?"

"It looks like we have a mystery to solve," said
Fred. "But we can't hang around," said Shaggy.
"It's closing time."
"Ret's ro!" Scooby agreed.

"Hmm," said Daphne. "Would you stay for a Scooby Snack?"

"Awhooo!" Howling filled the hall.

"Rikes!" cried Scooby. "A ronster." He jumped into Shaggy's arms.

"How about two Scooby Snacks?" asked Velma.

"Rokay!"

"Great," said Velma.
"Now, let's split up and look for clues," said Fred. "Daphne, Velma and I will find the security guard. He might know something."

Scooby and Shaggy headed down a long, dark hall. With every footstep they heard strange animal sounds. Then they heard a low, loud moan coming from behind a door. A sign on the door read KEEP OUT.

KEEP OUT

MUSEUM WORKERS ONLY

"Zoinks! It's a jungle beast!"
Shaggy yelped.

Shaggy and Scooby raced back
the other way and crashed right
into Velma, Fred and Daphne.
"There's a monster behind that
door! The sign says KEEP OUT.
And, like, that's what I want to do!"
Shaggy cried.

"I have an idea," Velma said.
She flung open the door.
Then she flipped on the light.

"Thank goodness!" said a voice.

"Hey, it's the security guard," said Shaggy.

"What are you doing here?" The guard waved his arms around the room. The gang saw buttons and levers and switches. "This is the museum control room," he explained.

"I thought so," said Velma. "I bet you stepped inside to close down the museum. But you couldn't see very well."

"I turned off the lights by accident," said the guard. "And when I tried to find the switch, I pressed all the wrong buttons."

With some help from the gang, the guard quickly
fixed everything. The museum grew quiet. Then
came a long, loud rumbling sound. Everyone jumped.
"That's just Scooby's tummy!" said Shaggy. "Hey,
can you flip one switch back on? The one for the
cafeteria?"

"Scooby-Dooby-Doo!" howled Scooby.

The Mystery Machine bumped along a dark,
empty road.
"Like, we're in the middle of nowhere!" said
Shaggy. "I hope we have enough gas!"
All at once, the van stopped.
"Roh-oh!" said Scooby.

"Engine trouble. We have to call a tow truck,"
said Fred. Velma and Daphne looked around.
Where could they find a telephone?
"Rook!" Scooby cried, pointing. "A right!"
"Maybe it's a house with a phone," said Velma.
"And a fridge," Shaggy added.

The gang walked towards the light.
It was growing brighter and brighter.
They were getting closer.
Suddenly, Velma said, "Jinkies!
It's not a house. It's a castle!"
The castle looked really spooky.
Scooby dug in his paws. He didn't
want to move.

"Come on, old buddy," Shaggy said. "Think
fridge! Think snacks!"
In a flash, Scooby swam across the moat and
banged on the drawbridge with his tail.

The drawbridge dropped. There were three
suits of armour stood at the door.
"Cool statues," said Shaggy.
"Clank, clank." The helmets snapped open.
They weren't suits of armour. They were
knights. Shiny spooky knights!

"Come on," said Fred. "We have to find a phone."

Scooby shook his head. "Ro way."

"For a Scooby Snack?" Velma asked.

Shaggy, Fred and Scooby raced inside.

In the castle's great hall, a chandelier swung back and forth. "Creak, creak."
"That's funny," said Daphne. "There's no breeze. What is making it move?"

"Ghosts!" whispered Scooby as a strange man rushed into the room. As the man opened his mouth to speak, Scooby saw his sharp, pointy teeth. "Rangs!" said Scooby.

"He's a vampire!" Shaggy cried, running away.

"Like, since we're running…" Shaggy said,
"let's run to the kitchen."
"Reah!" said Scooby.
In the kitchen, they saw a woman.
She stirred a big pot that bubbled over a fire.

"A witch!" cried Shaggy.

"You two are perfect!" said the witch. "Just what I need."

"No way," said Shaggy. "We're not part of your spooky recipe!"

Shaggy and Scooby
quickly raced away.
"Stop!" cried the witch.
"Stop!" cried the
vampire as they
chased Shaggy and
Scooby.

Shaggy and Scooby backed into a corner.
Suddenly, a mummy leapt up.
"Time is up!" he shouted.
"Our time is up, Scoob," Shaggy wailed.
"We've got to get out of here!"

They raced up the stairs.
"Stop!" cried the mummy.
"Stop!" cried the witch.
"Stop!" cried the vampire.
"Let's find Velma, Fred and
Daphne. Then we'll get outta
here," said Shaggy.

Finally, Shaggy flung open a door. Down
below, they saw monsters and zombies and
ghosts…

…and Velma, Daphne and Fred!
A knight was standing over them. He held his
sword tight.

"What should we do?"
Shaggy asked Scooby.
Just then the vampire,
witch and mummy
moved closer to them.

"Rump!" said Scooby.
"Jump?" Shaggy yelled.
Shaggy grabbed the chandelier.
Scooby grabbed Shaggy.
They swung across the room.

Shaggy and Scooby dropped to the floor...
right on top of the knight!
"My sword!" the knight cried.
"Grab it, Fred!" Shaggy shouted.
Fred scooped it up. But then he gave it back to
the knight!

Scooby hid his eyes. He was afraid to look.

"Relax," Velma said. "The knight is going to cut the cake."

Velma stepped out of the way. Now Shaggy
could see a party cake!
"It's a costume party!" Velma said.
"But," said Shaggy, "what about the ghostly
chandelier?"

"I was pulling a string," said the vampire,
"to move the chandelier into place."
"And the witch's potion?" Shaggy asked.
"Punch!" said the witch. "I wanted you to
try it."

"And the mummy's warning, 'Time is up'?"
The mummy smiled, "My nap time was over!"
"But you chased us!" said Shaggy.
"To invite you to the party," said the vampire.
"Uh, we knew it all along, right, Scooby?"
said Shaggy. "We were just acting."

Scooby looked around at all the smiling faces.
He stood up and bowed. "Scooby-Dooby-Doo!"
"Would you like to use the phone now?" asked
the knight.
"Uh, no rush," said Shaggy. "How about a nice
big piece of that cake?"

Shaggy, Scooby and the gang were at the Coolsville Bake-Off Contest.

"Like, get a noseful of that!" said Shaggy as he and Scooby sniffed the air.

"Rmmm-rmmm!"

Scooby and Shaggy had entered the contest.
They were going to bake Scooby Snacks.
"Like, this is the best!" Shaggy smiled.
"And the winner gets free pizza for a year!"

Velma, Fred and Daphne grabbed the supplies.
"These bags weigh a ton!" Velma said.
"What's in here?" asked Daphne.
"Ingredients," said Shaggy. "Flour, sugar… "
Then Scooby pulled out a box.
"Rizza!" Scooby cried.

"There's no pizza in Scooby Snacks,"
Velma said.
Shaggy took a big cheesy bite.
"It's not for the snacks," he explained.
"It's for the cooks!"
"Rat's right!" said Scooby.

"Humph!" said skinny Ms Pinchface, in the next booth. "What noisy eating!"
Shaggy and Scooby watched Ms Pinchface wash beans for a veggie pie. Then they spied the Tubb Twins making double fudge brownies. "Like, let's get cooking!" said Shaggy.

Scooby took out more ingredients. Then they pulled out baking sheets, dough cutters, chef hats, aprons, and finally: another pizza! "Whew!" Shaggy yawned. "I'm tired. If I weren't hungry for Scooby Snacks, I would take a nap. Like, let's hurry, Scoob. So we can snooze!"

Shaggy grabbed the flour. "Whoosh!" It
spilled on the floor. Scooby grabbed the eggs.
"Crack!" They smashed on the table.
"Pour!" Shaggy shouted. "Knead! Mix!"

Finally the dough was ready.
Shaggy and Scooby shoved the
snacks into the oven. In a flash,
they fell asleep.
Across the room, Velma, Fred
and Daphne heard a scream and
a thud.

It was Ms Pinchface, a bag of beans at her feet.
"What's wrong?" cried Daphne.
"There's a monster!" Ms Pinchface shouted.
"Over by my table! It's all white and spooky-looking, without any eyes!"

A rumbling noise shook the room. "I see
something on the other side!" Daphne cried.
"Let's go!" said Fred.
Velma, Fred and Daphne ran closer. The noise
grew louder.

But as they reached the cooking
booth, the noise had stopped.
The monster was gone.
"Like, quiet down, you guys,"
Shaggy said. "We're sleeping
here!"

"We're sorry," said Daphne. "But Ms Pinchface saw a monster!"
"A monster?" Shaggy said. "Wake up, Scooby. There's a monster…"
"Bing!" The oven timer went off.
"Ronster!" said Scooby, jumping up.

"That was the oven," said Velma. Shaggy opened the oven door carefully. "Zoinks!" cried Shaggy. "It's empty!" "No Rooby Racks?" said Scooby. "The monster ate your snacks!" said Ms Pinchface.

"Look at this!" said Velma. She pointed to handprints on the oven door… yellow ones!
"And rook!" cried Scooby. There were huge paw prints on the floor. Monster prints!
"Let's look for clues!" said Fred.
"Scooby and Shaggy can guard the oven," Velma said.

"Not even for free pizza!" Shaggy said, terrified.

"Would you do it for Scooby Snacks?" Velma asked.

Scooby sniffed hungrily. So did Shaggy. "Rooby Racks? Rokay!"

Velma, Daphne and Fred followed the trail of paw prints.

Shaggy and Scooby were alone. All at once,
they spied a trail of crumbs.
"This could lead to the monster!" said Shaggy.
"Or more Rooby Racks!" said Scooby.
They followed the crumbs.

Scooby licked up one crumb, then another. "Hey!" said Shaggy. "Leave some for me." He gobbled some up, too. "Slurp, slurp." They kept their heads to the ground. "Bump!" They crashed into Daphne, Fred and Velma.

Shaggy rubbed his head.
"Like, hey! We're back where we started. And so are you!"
"The crumbs circle the oven, and so do the paw prints," said Velma.

She peeked at Scooby's paws. "White!" said Velma. Next she looked at Shaggy's hands. "Yellow!" she cried. Fred wiped crumbs from Shaggy's shirt.

"These are like the ones on the floor!" he said.

"Shaggy, did you eat the Scooby Snacks?"
"Well, maybe I woke up from my nap for a minute, and ate some."
"What about you, Scooby-Doo?" Velma said.
Scooby shrugged. "I rate rome, roo."

"There is no monster!" Velma said. "We saw something white. But it was only Shaggy and Scooby in an apron and hat! Shaggy's hands are yellow from the egg yolk. He made the handprints! And Scooby's paws are white from flour. He made the paw prints! You both ate the snacks. And you didn't even know it!"

"Oh no! That means we are out of the contest," said Shaggy.
"Now you can try all the other food!" said Velma.
Shaggy took a bite of the veggie pie. "Like, this is delicious!" He eyed all the tables.
"And we've only just begun!" Scooby grinned. "Scooby-Dooby-Doo!"

"Like, any pizza around here?" said Shaggy.

"I'm starving."

"Rizza! Rizza!" Scooby said.

The rest of the gang laughed.

"There's no pizza here." Velma giggled.

"This is an apple orchard," Fred added.

"That's right," said Daphne. "We're here to pick apples."

"We're here to *pick* apples?" Shaggy moaned. "Not eat them?"

"That comes later," Daphne promised.

"Like, I'm so hungry," Shaggy said. "I'm going
to pick more apples than anyone!"
"Don't be so sure." Velma smiled. "I've read
books about how to pick apples . . ."
Shaggy looked at her. He was much taller than
Velma was. He could reach more apples.
"Let's have a contest," he said.

"We can split into groups. And the winners get to eat all the apples!" Shaggy continued. Shaggy pictured apple pies and apple jam. Scooby pictured toffee apples and sweet apple sauce. "Rapple sauce . . ." Scooby mumbled.

"Then let the contest begin!" said Velma. Everyone took baskets. Shaggy and Scooby went one way. Daphne led Fred and Velma the other way.

Shaggy reached for apples way up high.
Scooby bent for apples way down low.
One by one, they put them with care in
the basket.

A little later, Shaggy checked the basket.
"Zoinks!" he cried. "It's empty!"
Shaggy eyed Scooby. "Did you eat all the apples?"
"Ro ray," said Scooby. "Rou ate the rapples!"
"Like, no way for me, too!" Shaggy said.

They both shrugged. "Let's start over,"
said Shaggy.
They reached and pulled and picked and
tossed. Shaggy peeked in the basket.
Empty again!

"Scooby, stop eating the apples!" Shaggy cried.
Scooby shook his head. "Rou rop eating!"
"*You're* not eating the apples," said Shaggy.
"And *I'm* not eating the apples. So who's eating
the apples?"

All at once, Scooby shivered. It was getting
cold. The sun was going down.
They needed apples to win the contest. But
the apples kept disappearing!
"We have to figure this out," said Shaggy.
"Before it is too late."

"Who did this?" Shaggy called out.
"Who?" A voice called back.
Shaggy and Scooby jumped. Someone was teasing them. But they couldn't see anybody.

"We should call the police!" said Shaggy.
"*Call!*" said a voice.
They peered into the darkness. Still no one.
"Someone is out there," Shaggy said. "But he
must be invisible!"

All of a sudden, apples hit Shaggy and Scooby on the head.

"Ouch!" cried Shaggy.

"Rouch!" Scooby barked.

"It's an apple attack!" Shaggy screamed. "Run for your life, Scoob old buddy."

They turned to speed away. But they slipped on
wet leaves.

"Crash!" They bumped into something . . .
big . . . tall . . .

Giant arms trapped them.

"It's the invisible man!" Shaggy shouted.

"Boom! Boom!" They heard thudding
footsteps. Breaking branches. But they
couldn't see a thing. More invisible people!
"It's a whole army!" Shaggy wailed. "We're
goners!"

"Jinkies!" said a voice. "We finally found you!"
"The invisible man sounds just like Velma!"
said Shaggy.
Velma pulled a wet leaf from Shaggy's eyes.
"It *is* Velma," she said.

"What?" Shaggy leaped to his feet. "You're all here! You must have scared away the invisible men."

Shaggy explained about the missing apples. The voices teasing them. The apples hitting them on the head. The giant arms grabbing them.

Velma pushed away two branches. "These are
your giant arms. You ran into a tree. But you
couldn't tell because leaves covered your eyes."

"Who! Call!" the voices said again.
"Hmm," said Velma. "That 'whoooo'
sounds like a hoot. And the 'call'? That
sounds like *caw*."
"An owl and a crow!" Daphne exclaimed.

Next, Velma picked up the basket. "Aha! There's a hole in it! That's why the apples disappeared. They kept falling out!"

"But what about the apple attack?" Shaggy asked as another apple hit his head. "Ouch!" Fred grinned. "The apples are ripe."

"That's right," Velma agreed. "The wind blows them down. Or they fall down on their own."

The mystery was solved. But now it
was so dark, the gang could hardly see.
"How will we find our way back?"
asked Daphne.

"Look at this, Scoob!" said Shaggy. "All our apples! In a row!"

"It's like a trail," said Velma. "We can follow the apples to find our way back."

"But," said Shaggy, "how do we know who won the contest?"
Velma grinned. "You can walk, eat and count at the same time."
"One." *Crunch.* "Two." *Crunch.*
"Scooby-Dooby-Doo!"